Notes for Parents

The stories in this delightful picture book are ones which your child will want to share with you many times.

All the *Farmyard Tales* stories have been written in a special way to ensure that young children succeed in their first efforts to read.

To help with that success, first read the whole story aloud and talk about the pictures. Then encourage your child to read the short, simpler text at the top of each page and read the longer text at the bottom of the page yourself. Taking turns with reading builds up confidence and children do love joining in. It is a great day when they discover that they can read a whole book for themselves.

The *Farmyard Tales* series provides an enjoyable opportunity for parents and children to share the excitement of learning to read.

Betty Root

The Usborne Book of
FARMYARD TALES

Heather Amery
Illustrated by Stephen Cartwright

Edited by Jenny Tyler
Language Consultant: Betty Root

Cover Design by Doriana Berkovitch

There is a little yellow duck to find on every page

PIG GETS STUCK

This is Apple Tree Farm.

This is Mrs. Boot, the farmer. She has two children, called Poppy and Sam, and a dog called Rusty.

On the farm there are six pigs.

The pigs live in a pen with a little house.
The smallest pig is called Curly.

It is time for breakfast.

Mrs. Boot gives the pigs their breakfast.
But Curly is so small, he does not get any.

4

Curly is hungry.

He looks for something else to eat in the pen.
Then he finds a little gap under the wire.

Curly is out.

He squeezes through the gap under the wire.
He is out in the farmyard.

He meets lots of other animals in the farmyard.
Which breakfast would he like to eat?

Curly wants the hens' breakfast.

He thinks the hens' breakfast looks good.
He squeezes through the gap in the fence.

Curly tries it.

The hens' food is so good, he gobbles it all up.
The hens are not pleased.

Mrs. Boot sees Curly.

Curly hears Mrs. Boot shouting at him.
"What are you doing in the hen run, Curly?"

10

He runs to the fence.

He tries to squeeze through the gap. But he has eaten so much breakfast, he is too fat.

Curly is stuck.

Curly pushes and pushes but he can't move.
He is stuck in the fence.

They all push.

Mrs. Boot, Poppy and Sam all push Curly.
He squeals and squeals. His sides hurt.

Curly is out.

Then, with a grunt, Curly pops through the fence.
"He's out, he's out," shouts Sam.

14

He is safe now.

Mrs. Boot picks up Curly. "Poor little pig," she says. And she carries him back to the pig pen.

Curly is happy.

"Tomorrow you shall have lots of breakfast," she says. And Curly was never, ever hungry again.

16

THE NAUGHTY SHEEP

This is Apple Tree Farm.

This is Mrs. Boot, the farmer. She has two children, called Poppy and Sam, and a dog called Rusty.

On the farm there are seven sheep.

The sheep live in a big field with a fence around it.
One sheep has a black eye. She is called Woolly.

Woolly is bored.

Woolly stops eating and looks over the fence.
"Grass," she says, "nothing but grass. Boring."

Woolly runs out of the gate.

She runs out of the field into the farmyard. Then she runs through another gate into a garden.

Woolly sees lots to eat in the garden.

She tastes some of the flowers. "Very good,"
she says, "and much prettier than grass."

Can you see where Woolly walked?

She walks around the garden, eating lots of the flowers. "I like flowers," she says.

23

Mrs. Boot sees Woolly in the garden.

"What are you doing in my garden?" she shouts.
"You've eaten my flowers, you naughty sheep."

Mrs. Boot is very cross.

"It's the Show today," she says. "I was going to
pick my best flowers for it. Just look at them."

It is time for the Show.

"Come on," says Poppy. "We must go now. The Show starts soon. It's only just down the road."

They all walk down the road.

Woolly watches them go. She chews her flower and thinks, "I'd like to go to the Show."

Woolly goes to the Show.

Woolly runs down the road. Soon she comes to a big field with lots of people in it.

Woolly goes into the ring.

She pushes past the people and into the field.
She stops by a man in a white coat.

Mrs. Boot finds her.

"What are you doing here, Woolly?" says Mrs.
Boot. "She has just won a prize," says the man.

Woolly is the winner.

"This cup is for the best sheep," says the man.
"Oh, that's lovely. Thank you," says Mrs. Boot.

It is time to go home.

"Come on, Woolly," says Mrs. Boot. "We'll take you back to your field, you naughty, clever sheep."

BARN ON FIRE

This is Apple Tree Farm.

This is Mrs. Boot, the farmer. She has two children, called Poppy and Sam, and a dog called Rusty.

This is Ted.

Ted works at Apple Tree Farm. He looks after the tractor and all the other farm machines.

Poppy and Sam help Ted.

They like helping Ted with jobs on the farm. Today he is fixing the fence around the sheep field.

Sam smells smoke.

"Ted," says Sam, "I think something's burning."
Ted stops working and they all sniff hard.

The barn is on fire.

"Look," says Poppy, "there's smoke coming from the hay barn. It must be on fire. What shall we do?"

"Call a fire engine."

"Come on," says Ted. "Run to the house. We must call a fire engine. Run as fast as you can."

Poppy and Sam run to the house.

"Help!" shouts Poppy. "Call a fire engine.
Quickly! The hay barn is on fire."

Mrs. Boot dials the number.

"It's Apple Tree Farm," she says. "A fire engine please, as fast as you can. Thank you very much."

"You must stay here."

"Now, Poppy," says Mrs. Boot. "I want you and Sam to stay indoors. And don't let Rusty out."

Poppy and Sam watch from the door.

Soon they hear the siren. Then the fire engine roars up the road and into the farmyard.

"The firemen are here."

The firemen jump down from the engine.
They lift down lots of hoses and unroll them.

44

The firemen run over to the barn with the hoses.
Can you see where they get the water from?

The firemen squirt water onto the barn.

Poppy and Sam watch them from the window. "It's still burning on the other side," says Poppy.

"There's the fire."

One fireman runs behind the barn. What a surprise!
Two campers are cooking on a big wood fire.

The fire is out.

"We're sorry," say the campers. "It was exciting," says Sam, "but I'm glad the barn is all right."

THE RUNAWAY TRACTOR

This is Apple Tree Farm.

This is Mrs. Boot, the farmer. She has two children, called Poppy and Sam, and a dog called Rusty.

Ted is the tractor driver.

He has filled the trailer with hay. He is taking
it to the fields to feed the sheep.

Poppy and Sam hear a funny noise.

"Listen," says Sam. "Ted is shouting and the tractor is making a funny noise. Let's go and look."

They run to the top of the hill.

The tractor is racing down the hill, going faster and faster. "It won't stop," shouts Ted.

The trailer comes off.

The trailer runs down the hill and crashes into a
fence. It tips up and all the hay falls out.

The tractor runs into the pond.

The tractor hits the water with a great splash. The engine makes a loud noise, then it stops with a hiss.

Ted climbs down from the tractor.

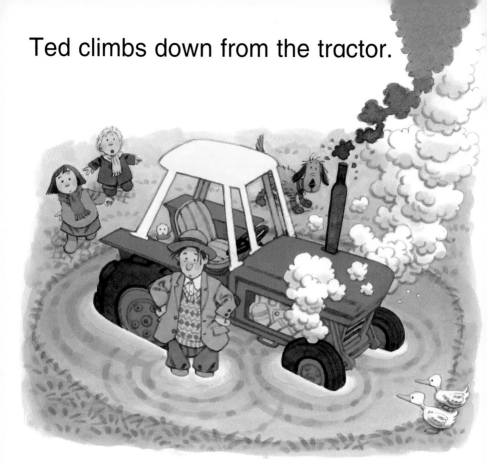

Ted paddles through the water and out of the pond. Poppy and Sam run down the hill.

Ted is very wet.

Ted takes off his boots and tips out the water.
How can he get the tractor out of the pond?

"Go and ask Farmer Dray to help."

"Ask someone to telephone Farmer Dray," says Ted. Poppy and Sam run off to the house.

58

Farmer Dray has a big horse.

Soon he walks down the hill with his horse.
It is a huge carthorse, called Dolly.

59

Ted helps with the ropes.

Farmer Dray ties the ropes to the horse. Ted ties
the other ends to the tractor.

Dolly pulls and pulls.

Very slowly the tractor starts to move. Ted pushes as hard as he can and Dolly pulls.

Ted falls over.

The tractor jerks forward and Ted falls in the water. Now he is wet and muddy all over.

The tractor is out of the pond.

"Better leave the tractor to dry," says Farmer Dray. "Then you can get the engine going again."

Poppy and Sam ride home.

Farmer Dray lifts them onto Dolly's back.
But Ted is so muddy, he has to walk.

This edition first published in 2001 by Usborne Publishing Ltd. Usborne House, 83-85 Saffron Hill,
London EC1N 8RT, England. www.usborne.com
Copyright © Usborne Publishing Ltd. 2000, 1999, 1989